Horoc... TWISTY TALES

The Three Frilly Goats Fluff

By Adam and Charlotte Gillain
and Phil Littler

W
FRANKLIN WATTS

This story is based on the traditional fairy tale,
The Three Billy Goats Gruff, but with a new twist.
You can read the original story in
Hopscotch Fairy Tales. Can you make
up your own twist for the story?

First published in 2012 by
Franklin Watts
338 Euston Road
London
NW1 3BH

Franklin Watts Australia
Level 17/207 Kent Street
Sydney
NSW 2000

Text © Adam and Charlotte Guillain 2012
Illustrations © Phil Littler 2012

The rights of Adam and Charlotte Guillain to be identified as the authors
and Phil Littler as the illustrator of this Work have been asserted
in accordance with the Copyright, Designs and Patents Act, 1988.

A CIP catalogue record for this book is available
from the British Library.
ISBN 978 1 4451 0671 7 (hbk)
ISBN 978 1 4451 0677 9 (pbk)

Series Editor: Melanie Palmer
Series Advisor: Catherine Glavina
Series Designer: Peter Scoulding

Printed in China

Franklin Watts is a division of
Hachette Children's Books,
an Hachette UK company
www.hachette.co.uk

Once upon a time there were
three Frilly Goats Fluff.

The three Frilly Goats Fluff wore frilly hats.

They wore frilly jumpers.

They wore frilly pants.

In fact EVERYTHING they wore looked frilly (and silly)!

The three Frilly Goats Fluff longed to go to the shops to buy more frilly things.

But there was a problem. A very big problem: the Troll.

The Troll lived under the bridge.

He was rough. He was tough.

He did all kinds of Troll-like stuff.

Especially eating goats

who crossed his bridge!

One day, the small Frilly Goat Fluff thought, "This scarf doesn't go with my top. I'm going to the shops."

She was scared of the Troll, but she really wanted a new scarf, so off she went.

"Who's that trip-trap-trapping over my bridge?" roared the Troll.

"Here, wear this!" bleated the small Frilly Goat Fluff. "You would look really nice in it." She threw her old scarf at the Troll.

The middle-sized Frilly Goat Fluff was trying on her old earrings. "These earrings are far too big for me," she sighed. "I need new ones."

She was scared of the Troll,
but she really wanted a new
pair of earrings, so off she went.

"Who's that trip-trap-trapping over my bridge?" roared the Troll. "Here, wear these!" bleated the middle-sized Frilly Goat Fluff. "They would look great with your scarf."

The middle-sized Frilly Goat Fluff
threw her earrings at the Troll.

The big Frilly Goat Fluff looked at her handbag. "This bag doesn't go with anything," she grumbled. "I'm going to the shops."

She was scared of the Troll, but she really wanted a new bag, so off she went.

"Who's that trip-trap-trapping over my bridge?" roared the Troll.

"Here, take this bag!" bleated the big Frilly Goat Fluff. "The colour matches your outfit." The big Frilly Goat Fluff threw her bag at the Troll.

The three Frilly Goats Fluff had
a great time at the shops.

Under the bridge, the Troll tried on all his new things.

"I like looking frilly," he said to himself. "I want more frilly things."

The three Frilly Goats Fluff finished shopping and walked home. When they got to the bridge, the Troll was waiting ...

... to show off his new clothes!

"You look great!" the three Frilly Goats Fluff said. "From now on, we'll all go shopping together!"

Puzzle 1

Put these pictures in the correct order.
Which event do you think is most important?
Now try writing the story in your own words!

Puzzle 2

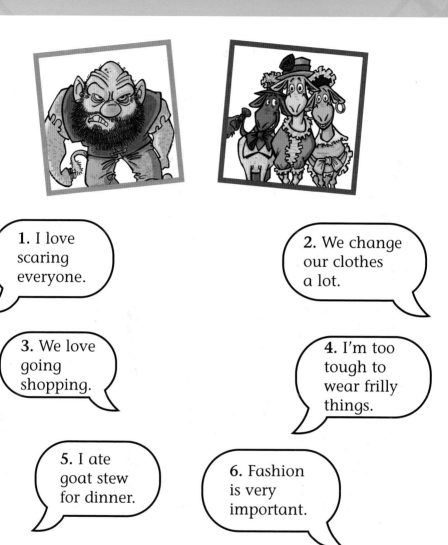

1. I love scaring everyone.

2. We change our clothes a lot.

3. We love going shopping.

4. I'm too tough to wear frilly things.

5. I ate goat stew for dinner.

6. Fashion is very important.

Choose the correct speech bubbles for each character. Can you think of any others? Turn over to find the answers.

Answers

Puzzle 1

The correct order is: 1a, 2f, 3e, 4b, 5d, 6c

Puzzle 2

The Troll: 1, 4, 5

The three Frilly Goats Fluff: 2, 3, 6

Look out for more Hopscotch Twisty Tales and Fairy Tales:

TWISTY TALES

The Princess and the Frozen Peas
ISBN 978 1 4451 0669 4*
ISBN 978 1 4451 0675 5

Snow White Sees the Light
ISBN 978 1 4451 0670 0*
ISBN 978 1 4451 0676 2

The Elves and the Trendy Shoes
ISBN 978 1 4451 0672 4*
ISBN 978 1 4451 0678 6

The Three Frilly Goats Fluff
ISBN 978 1 4451 0671 7*
ISBN 978 1 4451 0677 9

Princess Frog
ISBN 978 1 4451 0673 1*
ISBN 978 1 4451 0679 3

Rumpled Stilton Skin
ISBN 978 1 4451 0674 8*
ISBN 978 1 4451 0680 9

Jack and the Bean Pie
ISBN 978 1 4451 0182 8

Brownilocks and the Three Bowls of Cornflakes
ISBN 978 1 4451 0183 5

Cinderella's Big Foot
ISBN 978 1 4451 0184 2

Little Bad Riding Hood
ISBN 978 1 4451 0185 9

Sleeping Beauty – 100 Years Later
ISBN 978 1 4451 0186 6

FAIRY TALES

The Three Little Pigs
ISBN 978 0 7496 7905 7

Little Red Riding Hood
ISBN 978 0 7496 7907 1

Goldilocks and the Three Bears
ISBN 978 0 7496 7903 3

Hansel and Gretel
ISBN 978 0 7496 7904 0

Rapunzel
ISBN 978 0 7496 7906 4

Rumpelstiltskin
ISBN 978 0 7496 7908 8

The Elves and the Shoemaker
ISBN 978 0 7496 8543 0

The Ugly Duckling
ISBN 978 0 7496 8544 7

Sleeping Beauty
ISBN 978 0 7496 8545 4

The Frog Prince
ISBN 978 0 7496 8546 1

The Princess and the Pea
ISBN 978 0 7496 8547 8

Dick Whittington
ISBN 978 0 7496 8548 5

Cinderella
ISBN 978 0 7496 7417 5

Snow White and the Seven Dwarfs
ISBN 978 0 7496 7418 2

The Pied Piper of Hamelin
ISBN 978 0 7496 7419 9

Jack and the Beanstalk
ISBN 978 0 7496 7422 9

The Three Billy Goats Gruff
ISBN 978 0 7496 7420 5

For more Hopscotch books go to:
www.franklinwatts.co.uk

*hardback